THE THEA SISTERS

Nicky

She comes from Australia and is very enthusiastic about sports and nature. She loves being outside and is always ready to get up and go!

Pamela

She is a great mechanic: Give her a screwdriver and she'll fix anything! She loves pizza, which she eats every day, and she loves to cook.

D0179771

Do you want to help the Thea Sisters in this new adventure? It's not hard — just follow the clues!

When you see this magnifying glass, pay attention: It means there's an important clue on the page. Each time one appears, we'll review the clues so we don't miss anything.

ARE YOU READY?
A NEW MYSTERY AWAITS!

FIESTA IN MEXICO

Scholastic Inc.

If you purchased this book without a cover, you should be aware that this book is stolen property. It was reported as "unsold and destroyed" to the publisher, and neither the author nor the publisher has received any payment for this "stripped book."

Copyright © 2017 Edizioni Piemme S.p.A. International Rights © Atlantyca S.p.A., Via Leopardi 8, 20123 Milan, Italy; foreignrights@atlantyca.it, atlantyca.com English translation © 2022 by Atlantyca S.p.A.

The publisher does not have any control over and does not assume any responsibility for author or third-party websites or their content.

GERONIMO STILTON and THEA STILTON names, characters, and related indicia are copyright, trademark, and exclusive license of Atlantyca S.p.A. All rights reserved. The moral right of the author has been asserted. Based on an original idea by Elisabetta Dami. geronimostilton.com

Published by Scholastic Inc., *Publishers since 1920*, 557 Broadway, New York, NY 10012. SCHOLASTIC and associated logos are trademarks and/or registered trademarks of Scholastic Inc.

Stilton is the name of a famous English cheese. It is a registered trademark of the Stilton Cheese Makers' Association. For more information, go to stiltoncheese.com.

No part of this publication may be reproduced, stored in a retrieval system, or transmitted in any form or by any means, electronic, mechanical, photocopying, recording, or otherwise, without written permission of the copyright holder. For information regarding permission, please contact: Atlantyca S.p.A.

This book is a work of fiction. Names, characters, places, and incidents are either the product of the author's imagination or are used fictitiously, and any resemblance to actual persons, living or dead, business establishments, events, or locales is entirely coincidental.

ISBN 978-1-338-80222-1

Text by Thea Stilton
Original title *Viaggio in Messico*
Art director: Iacopo Bruno
Cover by Giuseppe Facciotto, Barbara Pellizzari, and Christian Aliprandi, and Flavio Ferron
Illustrations by Barbara Pellizzari, Valeria Brambilla, Chiara Balleello, Federico Giretti, Flavio Ferron, Tommaso Valsecchi Chiara Cebraro, and Antonio Campo
Graphics by Alice Iuri/theWorldofDOT

Special thanks to AnnMarie Anderson
Translated by Julia Heim
Interior design by Kay Petronio

10 9 8 7 6 5 4 3 2 1   22 23 24 25 26

Printed in the U.S.A.   40
First printing 2022

A COLORFUL EXIT!

It was a beautiful morning, and Mouseford Academy was buzzing with excitement. The students were about to leave for their winter VACATION.

As Colette finished packing her suitcase, she turned to her friend Pamela.

"What do you think today's **color** is, Pam?" Colette asked, her eyes twinkling.

Pamela laughed. Leave it to her stylish friend to ask a question like that!

Colette was passionate about **fashion**, and she loved anything to do with **color**: She was always up to date on the

hottest hues of the season, and she loved mixing clothes, bags, shoes, and bracelets to make unique outfits. Colette's LOVE for colors didn't stop there. The stylish mouselet had the fun habit of connecting colors to different memories and tasks. For example, a trip to the sea was the intense **BLUE** color of the waves mixed with the bright YELLOW of the sun. And, to Colette, an afternoon studying was brown and pink, like the tables in Mouseford Academy's library and her favorite notebook.

"Oh, there are so many colors for this morning!" Pamela replied. "There's the white of the SNOW outside, and the blue of my *passport* . . ."

"And the lilac on the cover of the latest issue of *Cosmouse* magazine," Colette added.

"Of course," Pamela agreed. "Let's not

forget the red from the **strawberries** in the muffins from breakfast!"

Colette smiled happily. "This morning is a r𝒶inbow of colors!"

At that moment, Violet, Paulina, and Nicky entered the room.

"Ready to go?" Violet asked.

There are so many colors!

Green!

"A-almost," Colette stammered as she lay on top of her **STUFFED** suitcase in an unsuccessful effort to close it.

Violet couldn't help but chuckle.

"When we said we would each bring just **ONE** suitcase, we meant we would also bring the amount of clothing that would fit in just **ONE** suitcase," Violet reminded Colette.

"Well, maybe I put a few extra things in here that I don't need . . ." Colette began. But before she had finished her sentence, she was interrupted by the **CLICK** of the suitcase lock as it latched shut. She quickly abandoned any thought of lightening her load.

"Perfect timing!" Colette rejoiced. "I'm all done. Now let's go!"

As the five friends headed out, they bumped into their friend Tanja.

"I'm so glad to see you!" the mouselet

exclaimed. "I really wanted to say good-bye."

"Where will you be spending your VACATION?" Violet asked.

"I'm going skiing with my parents," Tanja explained. "What about all of you?"

But just then, Colette's overstuffed suitcase popped open! CLICK!

Pamela burst out laughing and then immediately bent over to help her friend pick up the clothes and sandals that had scattered everywhere.

"Well, Colette's suitcase is a big clue," Tanja joked. "I'm guessing you're going somewhere WARM!"

"You're right!" Colette replied as she grabbed a straw hat and put it on her head. "We're going to Mexico!"

"Wow!" Tanja exclaimed. "I hear Mexico is beautiful. What part?"

"We are headed to the **Monarch Butterfly Biosphere Reserve** near Mexico City in Michoacán!" Paulina replied enthusiastically. "Dr. Meyer* invited us to join a group of

* DR. MAGGIE MEYER IS A MIGRANT BUTTERFLY SCHOLAR. THE THEA SISTERS WERE LUCKY ENOUGH TO MEET HER DURING A RESEARCH EXCURSION SHE TOOK TO WHALE ISLAND.

volunteers helping her team with a research project on monarch butterflies."

"I can't wait!" Nicky added enthusiastically.

"I can't wait either, but can you give me a few minutes before we head to the **AIRPORT**?" Colette asked sheepishly, her paws still full of the clothing that had escaped from her bag. "I'll be quick!"

I'm coming!

Without wasting another moment, Colette **DARTED** upstairs to the room she shared with Pam. She quickly tossed the clothes she wasn't taking on the bed and scampered back downstairs to join her **friends**.

As she hurried down, Colette smiled dreamily. She couldn't wait to get to **Mexico** — land of the bright, beautiful palette of the gorgeous monarch butterflies!

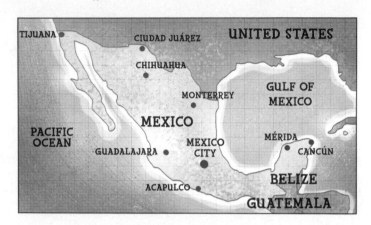

Mexico is a country in North America. It is located just south of the United States and northwest of Guatemala and Belize. The Pacific Ocean is to the west, while the Gulf of Mexico is to the east.

The **Mexican flag** is tricolored green, white, and red. The national coat of arms sits in the center of the flag. It is a golden eagle perched on a cactus holding a serpent in its talon.

Continent: North America   **Capital:** Mexico City
Official language: Spanish   **Currency:** Mexican peso

TRAVEL BUDDiES

The **Monarch Butterfly Biosphere Reserve** was located in the state of Michoacán, a few hours from Mexico City. Dr. Meyer had organized the trip for the mouselets, who would be joined by two volunteers from Mexico City. They were named Blanca and Mateo, and they had agreed to meet the mouselets at the airport to give them a ride to the reserve.

As they got off the plane, the five friends looked around for the two volunteers, but they didn't see anyone.

So the mouselets took advantage of the free time to change into lighter clothing now that they had left the cold weather on Whale Island behind them.

"I definitely won't need this while we're

here!" Pamela exclaimed happily as she stuffed her winter coat in her bag.

Once they had changed, the Thea Sisters headed outside the airport terminal to wait for their ride.

"How **fabumouse**!" Colette exclaimed as she stepped through the terminal's sliding doors, the soft, **warm** Mexican breeze ruffling her fur.

"I wonder where Blanca and Mateo are," Violet said, looking around. "I thought they were going to meet us here at the airport. I hope they didn't forget about us!"

Paulina glanced at the time. "Well, they aren't too late yet," she pointed out. "Maybe there was *traffic*."

"They should be about our age," Colette recalled from the professor's emails.

"Let's look around for them, then," Pamela

said as she **SCANNED** the crowd gathered outside the terminal. "Maybe they're waiting for us inside and we missed them."

"LOOK!" Violet exclaimed suddenly. "I think that might be them!"

The Thea Sisters turned to look in the direction Violet was pointing. Sure enough, a

Let's wait for them here.

Where could they be?

Maybe there was traffic . . .

van decorated with monarch butterflies was pulling up to the curb.

"You're right!" Nicky said as the van stopped in front of them.

"Sorry we're late!" a mouse with long brown hair called out from the passenger seat.

"You must be the Thea Sisters," the driver said WARMLY as the mouselets climbed into the van. "I'm Mateo."

"I'm Blanca," the first mouse added. "And it's all my fault we kept you waiting. I thought you'd be HUNGRY after your flight, so I started making *cocadas**, but then it got late!"

Blanca held out a basket of small golden treats to show them.

"Can you forgive us?" she asked.

Pamela took one whiff of the delicious coconut scent coming from the freshly baked cookies, and she broke into a grin.

_____

* *Cocadas* are a traditional coconut sweet.

They smell so good!

"Of course!" she squeaked happily. "For a snack like this, I would forgive you if you were ten hours late!"

Mateo steered the van back onto the road, and the group began their drive to ANGANGUEO, the small town where the volunteers would be staying during their visit. The Thea Sisters took advantage of the ride to get to know Blanca and Mateo better: In addition to their *love* of nature and animals, the mice had so many other things to chat about!

The Thea Sisters described their life at Mouseford Academy and explained how they had met Dr. Meyer while she was studying migrant butterflies on Whale Island. Then it was **Blanca** and **Mateo's** turn: The pair had known each other since they were young. In addition to being best friends, they went to school together, where they studied natural sciences and entomology.*

"So you'd both like to have careers like Dr. Meyer after you graduate," Paulina said.

Blanca smiled. "I wish!" she said. "It would be enough to be half as good as she is!"

"I'm sure you'll both make your dReaMS come true," Colette said encouragingly. "And then you'll both be entomologi-artists!"

Blanca raised her eyebrows. "Why **artists**?" she asked in surprise.

"Well, your van is painted so **beautifully**, I know one of you must be an artist!" Colette pointed out.

"Oh! That's our friend Luz's work," Mateo replied, smiling. "She studies art history at the

---

* Entomology is the branch of zoology that focuses on the study of insects, including butterflies.

university, and she's also a **talented** painter."

The mouselets enjoyed chatting with Mateo and Blanca so much that the ride flew by, and they reached Angangueo by sunset.

"Welcome!" Dr. Meyer greeted the group as they unloaded their bags. "It's such a pleasure to **see** you all!"

"The pleasure is all ours," Paulina assured her. "Thank you for inviting us!"

"Yes, thanks so much," Blanca added. "It's an **HONOR** for us to be here!"

"Oh, don't thank me — thank yourselves!" Dr. Meyer said, smiling. "I chose all of you because I know how hard you all work. Now, get settled and get some good rest because tomorrow will be a long day!"

A SPECIAL
WELCOME

The next morning, the mouselets were up early and were soon ready to go. Right after breakfast, Dr. Meyer explained their role in her research project.

"Over the next few days, we will be observing various colonies of monarch butterflies that have migrated to the reserve for the winter," she explained. "It will be your job to help out with data collection. You'll also guide the tourists visiting the reserve and make sure they don't interfere with our study."

"I can't wait!" Paulina whispered excitedly to Nicky.

"We'll leave in a few minutes to visit the first colony of butterflies," Dr. Meyer concluded.

As the mouselets prepared to head out for the day, Mateo and Blanca approached them.

"Good morning," Mateo greeted them warmly. "You're COMING with us, right?"

"Yes, of course!" the Thea Sisters replied happily. The five friends felt they had a lot in common with Blanca and Mateo, and they

The **Monarch Butterfly Biosphere Reserve** is in the state of Michoacán in central Mexico. Each fall, the monarch butterflies travel about 2,800 miles (4,500 km) from Canada and the United States to spend four to five months among the pine, oak, and oyamel fir trees of the Mexican forest.

were e×cited to spend more time getting to know their new friends.

"Then let's go!" Blanca said, and Colette, Nicky, Paulina, Pamela, and Violet followed her and Mateo.

We're going to see so many butterflies!

How cool!

The group began hiking along the trail that led through the forest where the monarch butterflies spent the winter.

"Isn't this amazing?" Colette asked Violet as the mouselets were immersed in the scents of the forest's plants and flowers. "I can't believe we're going to see butterflies that have traveled THOUSANDS of miles to get here."

"It's incredible," Violet agreed. "Especially since they didn't get to take a plane like we did: They flew here using tiny WINGS that are as thin as paper!"

"Their wings are delicate, but they're as strong as steel, too," Pamela pointed out. "Monarch butterflies are truly REMARKABLE creatures."

"It's true," Blanca agreed. "As soon as you set your EYES on the monarchs, you'll realize how SPECIAL they are. You won't be able to describe the emotion you'll feel!"

"So you've been here before?" Pamela asked.

"Yes, we've both been here MANY times," Mateo revealed. "In fact, this is where Blanca, Luz, and I met!"

Shhh . . .

Mateo stopped squeaking suddenly and turned to the Thea Sisters with a finger to his lips.

"What is it?" Nicky whispered softly.

Mateo **pointed** to a tree a little ways off the trail. At first the others thought the branches were covered in small orange-and-yellow leaves. But on closer inspection, the Thea Sisters realized they weren't leaves at all, but rather thousands and thousands of butterflies!

It was a truly REMARKABLE sight. In some spots, there were so many butterflies that their **weight** bent the branches they were sitting on!

"The butterflies gather close to one another to retain their body HEAT," Blanca explained softly. "Here in the mountains, the temperature can get very *cool* at night."

Wow!

"Are they sleeping?" Violet asked.

Mateo shook his head.

"During the chilly evening and morning hours, they rest and wait for the air temperature to **warm up**," he explained.

"How CLEVER!" Nicky exclaimed as she and the other Thea Sisters caught up with the rest of the researchers. They had stopped in a clearing SURROUNDED by trees that were completely covered with butterflies.

A moment later, the midmorning sun peered through the tops of the trees and flooded the clearing with rays of *LIGHT*. It was as if the butterflies had received a secret signal because they suddenly began to unfold their wings. Soon the sky filled with gold, black, and orange as the butterflies took flight. The flapping of millions of wings was reminiscent of the tapping of *rain* on a roof during a storm. Every one of the researchers stopped and stared up at the trees, *awestruck*.

The students and scientists knew they were there because they had a job to do. But at that moment, all they could do was stop and stare at the stunning monarchs that had taken to the skies as if to greet them and wave hello! The group was simply astounded by the incredible sight of

BUTTERFLIES FLYING ALL AROUND THEM!

An Invitation

Blanca had been **RIGHT**: It was hard to find the words to describe the **FEELING** of being surrounded by thousands and thousands of magnificent monarch butterflies.

But Paulina quickly found a way to capture and preserve the feeling: During the days she and the Thea Sisters spent with Dr. Meyer and her team, she took tons and tons of photographs!

Paulina had never been one to leave her camera behind, and it was paying off on this trip. After spending her days searching for marvemouse natural LANDSCAPES, Paulina would upload her photos to her laptop. Then the Thea Sisters, Blanca, Mateo, and the

MONARCHS LANDING
IN A BROOK

MONARCHS
IN FLIGHT

MONARCHS TAKING
A DRINK

other volunteers and researchers would gather around to admire her **photos**!

Before the end of the week, word of Paulina's talent as a photographer reached Dr. Meyer. One evening, the entomologist caught up with the Thea Sisters and their **friends** while they were **happily** looking at the day's photos.

"Can I join you?" the professor asked.

"Of course, have a seat!" the friends replied as they made room. Dr. Meyer sat next to Paulina.

"Are these the famouse photographs I've heard so much about?" she asked, smiling.

"**Famouse?!**" Paulina asked in surprise.

Dr. Meyer nodded. "Well, my colleagues have been talking about them: Everyone is impressed with your skill."

Paulina **blushed**.

"Thank you," she said shyly. "I haven't been

doing it very long, but I really enjoy photography."

"I would *love* to see more of your photos," the professor said. "May I?"

"Of course!" Paulina replied eagerly.

Dr. Meyer looked at the photographs Paulina

had taken over the past few days. The images told such a beautiful story about these butterflies.

"Paulina, these images are even more BEAUTIFUL than what was described to me," Dr. Meyer complimented the mouselet. "This is incredible work! In fact, your images are so remarkable that I would like to ask your **permission** to use them."

"USe them?!" Paulina asked in surprise. "Really?"

Well done!

Thank you!

The professor nodded. "Yes," she said. "I'm giving a talk at a **conference** next week in Mexico City. I'll be meeting with colleagues from all over the world, and I'll be telling them about the experience here at the reserve. Your photos would be the perfect **PAIRING** to my talk!"

"I would be honored!" Paulina replied. "I can share the files with you."

But the professor shook her head. "It would be better if you joined me," she explained. "That way you can tell everyone **how** you took these incredible shots. I think it would make the story of the reserve even more MEANINGFUL."

Then she turned to the other Thea Sisters. "All of you should come!" she said warmly.

The **five friends** looked at one another, stunned. It was an incredible opportunity.

"Thank you so much," Paulina *replied*, flattered. "But there's one problem: We already booked our tickets to return to Whale Island."

"You could change your reservation and **delay** your departure for a few days," Mateo suggested. "Or do you have to get back for the start of CLASSES immediately?"

Pamela shook her head. "No, once we get back, we still have a few days of **VACATION**," she said. "We would love to stay and support our friend, of course! But will we be able to find a hotel in Mexico City on such short notice?"

"Don't be silly, you don't need to reserve a hotel," Blanca said. "You can STAY with me!"

"Really?!" Nicky asked in surprise. "**All five of us?**"

"Of course!" Blanca said, smiling. "You'll be my guests. It will be tight, but that's part of the fun! This way you can **participate** in the conference and spend a few days visiting our beautiful city!"

"It seems like a perfect plan!" Mateo agreed.

Paulina LOOKED at her new friends in disbelief.

"You're all so kind," she said. "I don't know what to say!"

"I do," Dr. Meyer replied, smiling.

"Tell us you'll come!"

NICE TO MEET YOU, LUZ!

The decision had been made: The Thea Sisters would **stay** a few extra days in Mexico as guests of their new friend Blanca. So the next day, the mouselets packed their suitcases, said good-bye to everyone at the butterfly reserve, and climbed aboard Blanca and Mateo's van. They were headed to **Mexico City**!

A short while later, Mateo pulled off the highway and turned the van down a street that led to a quiet Residential area. He stopped in front of a white building with a balcony decorated with pots of **BRIGHT RED** geraniums.

"How pretty!" Colette exclaimed, admiring the colorful alley. "This street looks like it's right off a postcard!"

"Welcome to my home!" Blanca exclaimed. Then she opened the **wooden** door and led the way upstairs. "My parents are away visiting my **grandmother**, so I thought I'd stay in their room.

Welcome to my home!

What beautiful flowers!

Some of you can sleep in my bedroom, and some in the living room. Does that work?"

"That would be perfect," Violet assured her. "Thank you so much for your hospitality!"

"I'll leave you all to RELAX and get settled —" Mateo began, before he was interrupted by his phone *buzzing*. He glanced down at the message and read it. Then he broke into a huge grin. "Actually, forget what I just said. Let's head out right away: Luz can't wait to meet all of you!"

The group headed straight to Plaza Garibaldi to meet up with Blanca and Mateo's friend. When they arrived, they were charmed by the plaza's festive atmosphere.

"What lively music!" Nicky exclaimed as she and her friends were surrounded by three mice in suits and sombreros who were singing and playing instruments.

"They're mariachi players," Mateo told the Thea Sisters. "They specialize in traditional Mexican music."

"It really makes me want to DANCE!" Paulina exclaimed as she and the others made their way through the square, which was full of musicians performing and entertaining the crowds.

Then, suddenly, a bright, happy voice called out over the music: "Hi, mouselets!"

"Here's Luz!" Blanca exclaimed, running to hug her friend.

"What a pleasure to meet all of you!" Luz said once she had been introduced to the Thea Sisters. "These past few days, Blanca and Mateo have sent me a ton of messages telling me about these AMAZING mice they met at the reserve!"

The group *headed* toward a block-long

building with a sign outside that read MERCADO SAN CAMILITO.

Inside they found more mariachi groups, COLORFUL garlands hanging from the ceiling, and dozens of food stalls selling traditional Mexican foods.

"OH, WOW!" Pamela exclaimed. "How will I ever decide what to try? I know: I'll close my eyes and follow the scent I like the most!"

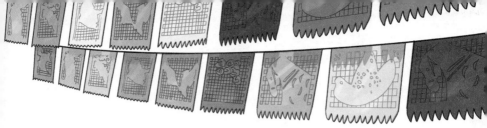

Blanca, Luz, and Mateo just laughed.

"Then we'll let you lead the way!" Mateo said.

Pamela led the group to a vendor who served stuffed corn tortillas called **enchiladas**. They all sat down to enjoy their food while getting to know Luz better.

"Blanca and Mateo told us you're the one who painted the beautiful butterflies on their van," Paulina said to Luz. "You're really talented!"

"Thank you," Luz replied, smiling. "When we decided to decorate the van, I had no doubt about what I wanted to paint: You could say that monarch butterflies are the symbol of our friendship!"

The three friends explained that years earlier

they had met at the **Monarch Butterfly Biosphere Reserve**.

"We were kids, and we had each gone there on trips with our families," Blanca explained. "The three of us found ourselves standing there side by side as we listened to the tale of the monarchs' migration."

"The story of the long JOURNEY of the butterflies captured my **heart**," Luz said dreamily. "It's incredible that they can travel so far — to a place they've never been —

guided only by iNStiNCt. And then they return home months later!"

"That's when we became friends," Mateo added. "We discovered that we were all from the same city, and we started to hang out. But each time we have the chance, we return to the reserve. Blanca and I have become more and more interested in studying butterflies, while Luz loves drawing them!"

"What a beautiful story," Pamela said as she took a corn chip and dunked it in a spicy avocado dip called *guacamole*.*

"So, Luz is the artist, while Blanca and Mateo are the scientists," Colette observed in admiration.

GUACAMOLE

"Luz is an artist *and* an expert in the wonders of Mexico City!" Blanca clarified.

---

* *Guacamole* is a Mexican dish made of mashed avocado with chopped onion, tomatoes, chili peppers, and seasoning.

"You two know the city really well, too," Luz replied, SMILING.

"Of course we do," Mateo said, chuckling. "But that's because we never miss any of your **fascinating** tours!"

"Tours?" Violet asked, curious. The Thea Sisters discovered that Luz *loved* history as well as art, and she especially enjoyed sharing the wonders of her hometown with others. Because of this, Luz was a volunteer guide through her school. She and the other members of her group offered walking tours of the most picturesque parts of Mexico City.

"There's nothing I like more than a long walk around an **EXCITING** new city!" Nicky exclaimed. "I would love to go on one of your tours."

"Me, too," Colette agreed. "That would be incredimouse. Is there any chance you're leading a tour that we could join tomorrow?"

"No, I'm sorry," Luz said, disappointed. "I have other plans tomorrow."

Then she broke into a grin. "I'm just kidding!" she squeaked, laughing. "Tomorrow I'll be the guide on a very special private tour around the city, just for the **FIVE OF YOU**!"

I'll be your guide!

LET THE TOUR BEGIN!

The next morning, Luz, Blanca, Mateo, and the Thea Sisters gathered outside in front of Blanca's house.

"**Are you ready?**" Luz asked.

"We sure are!" Pam responded. "We loaded up on *huevos rancheros** at breakfast, and we all have our walking shoes on. Let's go!"

The itinerary Luz had planned for the morning would lead the group through the historic center of **Mexico City**.

Their first stop was the Palacio de Bellas Artes, the city's famous concert hall and arts center.

---

* *Huevos rancheros* is a Mexican breakfast of fried eggs served on tortillas and topped with a *salsa fresca* of tomatoes, peppers, onions, and cilantro.

Luz led the Thea Sisters inside, where they admired COLORFUL *murales* — murals by the famouse Mexican painters Diego Rivera and David Alfaro Siqueiros. She explained that the *elegant* white building housed the **largest** theater in the country, which was a venue for classical music concerts, operas, symphonies, and dance performances. Because she was a guide, Luz was able to give them a **PEEK** inside the theater, which was usually only visible during shows.

"Is that **CURTAIN** made of glass?!" Paulina asked

in disbelief as she took in the stage's remarkable backdrop.

"It is!" Luz replied. "The stained-glass panels were created by New York jeweler Tiffany & Co. using nearly a million pieces of colored GLASS!"

"The glass mosaic depicts a landscape of the Valley of Mexico," Mateo added. "In the center you can see the Popocatépetl and Iztaccíhuatl volcanoes."

"With a backdrop like this, you almost don't need any shows!" Nicky remarked.

"It's true!" Luz agreed as they left the theater. "And now on to the *second stop* on our tour — the skyscraper Torre Latinoamericana, or Latin American Tower!"

They rode the elevator to the forty-fourth floor of the building, where the observation deck offered panoramic views of the entire city.

Once they got back

down to street level, they continued their walk through the historic center until they reached the **Plaza de la Constitución**.

"This is the most important and beloved square in Mexico City," Luz explained as she stood beneath the huge tricolored Mexican flag that waved from the central **FLAGPOLE**. "Locals call it El Zócalo. It's also one of the largest squares in the world. And there is the Palacio Nacional — the presidential palace!"

Luz led the group inside, where they admired the gardens and the majestic murals that depicted the history of Mexico.

"This city is full of art," Violet reflected as the group returned to El Zócalo. "It's incredible that over the centuries artists have decorated both interior walls and the walls outside city buildings. Now locals and tourists

can enjoy a little bit of beauty every day!"

"Violet's right," Colette agreed. "Mexico City is like an open-air painting, and

It's all so colorful!

You'll see even more at our next stop!

it's the most COLORFUL painting I've ever seen!"

Luz's eyes lit up at Colette's words.

"I'm so happy you feel that way!" she gushed. "Now I can't wait to show you the next and final stop on our tour. It's my favorite place in the city, and it even has color in its name: La Casa Azul!"

THE BLUE HOUSE

La Casa Azul means The Blue House, and the Thea Sisters could see why it was called that: The building was painted an electric blue both outside and in! But La Casa Azul wasn't just blue: There were touches of bright yellow, green, and red everywhere, making the place truly unique.

"This was the childhood home of the great Mexican painter **FRIDA KAHLO**," Luz explained. "She is most known for her remarkable self-portraits. This house is also where she learned to paint and produced most of her work."

"And it was turned into a **mouseum**?" Violet asked, fascinated.

"That's right," Luz confirmed. "Today it is a mouseum where visitors can admire Frida's

paintings and immerse themselves in the details of her everyday life."

The group walked through the MULTICOLORED rooms and observed each detail of the places where the artist had painted, slept, cooked, and lived. They stopped in the kitchen, where the yellow of the floor, the table, the chairs, and the sideboard matched the yellow details on the blue tiles. Then they continued into the bedroom, where **FRIDA KAHLO** spent much of her life painting from her bed after an accident left her injured and in poor health.

As they made their way through her studio, they took in the views outside the large windows. They marveled at the tidy rows of colorful paints, palettes, and sketchbooks that the artist had used, which had all been perfectly **preserved**. After taking in Frida's private rooms, the group moved on to a room where the painter's works were exhibited along with COLORFUL clothing that she had *loved* to wear.

"Are you okay, Colette?" Pamela asked her friend as they headed out into the gardens. "You seem a little quiet."

"I don't know how to explain it, but I feel so enchanted by Frida's world of colors!" Colette exclaimed. "She was such an inventive and original painter — it's as though the

different colors were the characters in her art. She seemed to bring COLOR into every part of her life. It's in every detail of her house, in the beautiful clothes she wore, and in the flowers and ribbons she put in her hair. She was a true artist!"

After walking through the green garden, the group stopped near a fountain.

"You're right, Colette," Luz agreed. "FRIDA also loved animals, and she transformed this garden into a kingdom where her four-legged friends ROAMED free. Sometimes I come here and imagine her as she walked among the plants looking for inspiration, followed by a dog, a monkey, or a parrot!"

"You really admire her, don't you?" Nicky asked Luz.

"She's much more than an admirer," Blanca said. "Why don't you tell the Thea Sisters about your project, Luz?"

Colette's ears perked up. "A project about Frida Kahlo?" she asked.

Luz quickly filled in her friends. She explained that she was participating in a show dedicated to Mexican art and culture that was being organized by the art history program at her school. Every student that participated must design an area inside the big pavilion. They each had to pick a *theme*, and Luz decided she would use her favorite artist as inspiration.

"I chose **FRIDA KAHLO**," Luz explained. "The show will be open to the public in a few days, and I'm working on the

final **details** now.
I hope it goes well!"

"Of course it will go well," Blanca assured her friend. "You've worked so hard and you are so

These colors are truly fabumouse!

talented. I'm sure the selection committee will notice!"

"There's a competition tied to the show," Mateo explained. "The student with the BEST PROJECT will win a scholarship to study abroad for a year."

"Wow!" Paulina exclaimed. "That would be incredimouse. You would learn so much."

"I can't wait for the opening to see what you created," Colette added.

"Actually, you can see it whenever you'd like," Luz said. "I'm still working on the finishing touches, but I would be *happy* to give you a preview. What do you say?"

"Yes!" the Thea Sisters squeaked at once.

"We would love that," Violet said.

"I can't wait to see your project, Luz," Colette added. "I just know it will fill my soul with many HAPPY COLORS!"

THE COMPETITION
HEATS UP

The next day, the Thea Sisters, Blanca, and Mateo had a plan to meet Luz to get a sneak peek at her **FRIDA KAHLO** project. Blanca and the Thea Sisters arrived right on time at the entrance to the exhibition pavilion. LUZ was waiting there happily for them.

"Good morning!" she greeted everyone. "I can't wait to *show you* everything. Let's head inside!"

"Shouldn't we wait for Mateo?" Nicky asked.

"Mateo got here a few minutes ago," Luz replied as she headed into the pavilion. "He offered to bring some of my canvases inside. He'll meet us at my stand."

The Thea Sisters entered the enormous room where the show would take place.

They walked past a number of students who were **working** hard on their pieces. One stand in particular caught Colette's eye.

"Oh, wow!" Colette exclaimed. "Look at this!"

She had stopped in front of a mannequin displaying a beautiful multicolored dress. Luz smiled.

Good morning!

"This project is dedicated to the traditional embroidered *clothing* Mexico is known for," she explained. "This is Susana's stand. She's my classmate and a volunteer tour guide, like me."

Just then a mouse with a not-so-friendly smile approached them.

"Hi, Luz," she said. "Are you looking for ideas to steal from your classmates?"

Luz smiled. "Umm, this is Susana, the creator of this beautiful project on Mexican fashion," Luz told the Thea Sisters.

"So nice to meet

Look!

I know I'll win!

you, Susana," Colette said quickly so Luz would feel less embarrassed by her classmate's rude greeting. "And compliments on such an original idea. I love fashion and I think it's amazing that someone included it among the other art forms!"

"Well, thank you," Susana replied proudly. Then she turned to Luz. "See? That's why I'm going to win the scholarship. After all, my idea is the most original!"

"Oh, we really have to go now!" Blanca cut in, dragging Luz and the Thea Sisters away before the situation got any worse.

"Someone should explain to Susana that she's not being a good sport at all!" Nicky remarked as soon as they had gotten far enough away.

"I know, she is always so rude," Luz said with a sigh. "Don't pay her any attention."

"I think I spotted your project, Luz!" Pamela exclaimed suddenly, pointing straight ahead. "That's the garden from La Casa Azul!"

The mouselets gathered around the beautiful backdrop for Luz's **project**. They admired the large painting, which was spread over four panels and was an exact depiction of the garden at **FRIDA KAHLO'S** Casa Azul.

"Did you paint the entire thing yourself?" Violet asked, stunned. "It's spectacular!"

Luz just nodded and smiled SHYLY.

"Great work assembling these panels, too," Pamela remarked. "It's very **WELL DONE!**"

"It was **EASIER** to transport it that way," Luz said. Then she explained the finishing touches she still had to add to the piece. "I'm planning to put some live plants in front of the background to better re-create the garden environment. The rest of the space will be full of easels, where I'll display paintings that tell the story of Frida Kahlo's life using photos and text."

"I'm sorry to interrupt, Luz, but there's something over here you should see," Pamela said. "Something isn't quite right here . . ."

Luz **hurried** over.

"What is it?" she asked, a worried look on her snout.

"It looks like this panel is about to come off," Pamela explained as she showed Luz one

of the panels, which was leaning at an **odd** angle and looked like it might fall.

"Pam's right," Paulina agreed as she stepped forward to examine the mechanism that held the panels together. "The screw is missing from this **hinge**."

"It's a good thing you noticed!" Luz said as she dug up another screw from a box of tools. "If this panel had fallen, it would have knocked over all the others. That would have been a real **disaster**!"

"I wonder what happened," Blanca said, confused. "The screw couldn't have FALLEN OUT on its own!"

"That's true," Luz agreed slowly. "I really don't know what **HaPPeNeD**. I was sure I tightened it correctly, but maybe not. Or the screw may have come LOOSE when I moved the panels."

"That would be odd, but not **IMPOSSIBLE**," Mateo said.

"True," Luz said as she placed the new screw in the hinge. "I'll be sure to pay close **ATTENTION** to what I'm doing!"

"And we're here if you *need* us," Paulina offered helpfully.

"Yes, if there's anything we can do, just let us know," Violet agreed, smiling warmly.

A FOREST
IN THE CITY

The Thea Sisters still had a few days to enjoy Mexico City before **Dr. Meyer's** conference began. They took full advantage of having *new friends* as their tour guides.

"Today I'll take you all for a walk in the woods!" Blanca announced at breakfast.

"That sounds fabumouse," Nicky agreed. "I'm always eager to explore nature. Will it take a long time to get there?"

"Not at all," Blanca replied, smiling. "The Bosque de Chapultepec — or Chapultepec Forest — is right here. It's a really unique forest in the middle of Mexico City!"

"Great!" Colette said eagerly. "Will Mateo and LUZ be coming with us?"

"Mateo, yes," Blanca replied. "And Luz will

meet up with us when she is done working on her **PROJECT**."

A short while later, everyone was ready to head out to explore the beautiful Chapultepec Forest — the enormouse **GREEN HEART** of Mexico City.

"What time did you say Luz would meet us?" Violet asked as the group wound their way among the cacti in the park's botanic garden.

Blanca glanced at the time on her phone.

"Actually, she should be here already," she replied. A second later, her phone RANG. "Oh, that's her now! Maybe she is looking for us."

But as the Thea Sisters watched Blanca take the call, the look on Blanca's snout changed. Something wasn't right.

"What happened?" Colette asked once Blanca had hung up the phone.

"Luz had a problem with her registration for the **show**," Blanca explained. "It seems she's **MISSING** one of the forms. If she doesn't get the paperwork in right away, she won't be able to **PARTICIPATE**!"

The group continued their tour of the Chapultepec Castle — an ancient building in the middle of the urban Chapultepec Forest.

It's Luz!

Is she coming?

Still, they kept thinking about Luz's problem. When they stepped out onto the castle's panoramic terrace overlooking the city, Blanca's phone **RANG** once again. It was Luz, and she was at the castle! A moment later, she caught up with the group.

"So did you solve the **PROBLEM** with your registration?" Paulina asked as the mouselets settled on a stretch of lawn near the **LAKE** so they could chat while snacking on some warm *churros.**

I did it!

"I got it done just in time!" Luz said, nodding. "I was sure that I had **filled** out that form and put it in the envelope with the others."

"You were with me and Mateo when you filled them out," Blanca

* *Churros* are long sticks of dough that are fried and dusted with cinnamon and sugar.

reminded Luz. "And you showed us the forms and asked us to double-check that you had completed everything. *Right, Mateo?*"

Mateo swallowed a big bite of churro.

"I think so, but I'm not sure," he replied. "I wouldn't **worry** about it now, though. It must have been the organization that lost the form. The important thing is that everything worked out."

"It's too bad you missed this morning's trip,

though," Nicky pointed out. She glanced at the LAKE and smiled. "What do you say we take a paddleboat ride?"

"That's a great idea!" Luz squeaked, jumping to her paws excitedly. "Come on, let's go!"

"I'm going to stay here," Mateo said as the others all stood. "I'm a bit tired. But you all should go ahead! You can leave your bags here with me."

Everyone agreed, and the mouselets waved good-bye to Mateo. The trip around the lake was fun and refreshing, and Luz was able to put aside thoughts about the hiccup with the registration forms. When they returned to shore, she was calm and collected again.

"That was such a good idea," Luz said as she sat down on the grass. "I feel really recharged. I'll take advantage of this energy to work on my project a bit."

Luz opened up her **LAPTOP** as her friends stretched out on the lawn to enjoy the last RAYS OF SUN.

A moment later, though, Luz looked worriedly at her laptop screen.

"But that's *not possible*!" she said. "The folder with all my material for the show DISAPPEARED! I lost everything!"

CLUE!
A FORM WAS MISSING FROM LUZ'S REGISTRATION DOCUMENTS FOR THE COMPETITION. HOW DID THAT HAPPEN?

THE FOLDER WITH LUZ'S FRIDA KAHLO PROJECT DISAPPEARED FROM HER COMPUTER. HOW?

THE MISSING FILE

After Luz realized the file was missing from her **computer**, the group quickly headed back to Blanca's house to plug in Luz's laptop and calmly assess the situation.

Luz had saved all the photos and text files that told the story of **FRIDA KAHLO'S** life in one folder on her computer. She was planning to exhibit the info on easels during the show.

"I worked on that for weeks!" Luz exclaimed as she paced back and forth while Paulina examined the laptop. "And now **everything** is gone!"

"Don't give up **HOPE**," Violet said, trying to console Luz as she passed her a cup of tea. "There must be another option."

Luz took a long sip.

"I'm really in TROUBLE," she said. "All the material that I planned to print and exhibit at the show was in that folder!"

"You didn't save a backup copy just to be safe?" Pamela asked.

Luz shook her head, **DISAPPOINTED**.

"Well, I did save a backup, but that was ten days ago," she admitted. "I've made so many changes and corrections, and I've added a lot of photos since then, too. What do I do **now**? It would take way too long to get everything back the way it should be. I'll have to pull out of the competition!"

"Let's put our snouts together," Colette said encouragingly. "I'm sure we can come up with another **solution**. What do you say, Paulina? You're our IT expert. Can you think of anything we can try?"

Paulina thought for a moment.

"Well, there is one thing," she said. "Luz, **WHERE** was the folder?"

"It was on the desktop, and it was called *Frida*," Luz replied. "Now it's gone, but I know I didn't move it. I'm always really careful about that."

"Got it." Paulina nodded, deep in her own thoughts. First, she OPENED the computer's **trash** folder, but it was empty. Next Paulina tried to *search* to see if the folder *Frida* had ended up somewhere else accidentally, but she couldn't find it anywhere.

Luz's eyes filled with tears.

"I don't believe it," she said. "I worked so hard on this project and now **ALL MY WORK IS GONE!**"

"Wait a minute," Paulina interjected. "That isn't necessarily true. There are computer programs that allow you to recover deleted files. I'll install one now and see if it helps. But it will take some time for the program to **LOAD**."

The group waited patiently while Paulina installed and then ran the **recovery** program. It was late in the evening when Paulina checked the **laptop** and squeaked with excitement.

"There it is!" she exclaimed. "We did it! We **RECOVERED** the folder with all your work in it, Luz!"

"You did?!" Luz gasped in surprise. Then she ran to hug Paulina. "My work is really saved?! *THANK YOU, THANK YOU!* I really don't know how to thank you!"

Paulina just *smiled*.

"It was my pleasure. And I know what you can do for me," she said. "Go get a good night's rest so you'll be well rested and in great shape for our **WALKiNG TOUR** tomorrow!"

CLUE!

LUZ SAID SHE DIDN'T ERASE THE FRIDA FOLDER... SO HOW DID IT DISAPPEAR?

THE PYRAMID
OF THE SUN

The trip planned for the following day was special because it was organized by the **WALKING TOUR** group Luz volunteered with, and it was open to a lot of tourists. It was a unique tour, too, as it included an HOUR-LONG bus trip to Teotihuacán, a vast archaeological site northeast of Mexico City.

"Wow!" Nicky exclaimed once they had reached their destination. "This morning we woke up in a city of skyscrapers, and now it's like we've gone back in time!"

"I can't wait to explore." Colette smiled. "And I can't wait to see Luz in action as an OFFICIAL tour guide!"

It didn't take Colette and the other Thea Sisters long to figure out that Luz the "official guide" wasn't really so different from the Luz who had taken the group of friends all around Mexico City. The mouselet had so much love for the history of her country, and she was able to convey it without being overly chatty or intrusive. Her stories were always told with care and had a unique way of sparking the imagination of the tourists who listened to them! Basically, Luz was a terrific guide.

Since the group was fairly large, there were two guides: LUZ and Susana, whom the Thea Sisters had met at the exhibition on Mexican culture.

Unfortunately, Susana seemed more intent on taking jabs at her colleague than on guiding the tourists through the ruins of the city.

"Are you sure you counted the participants correctly?" Susana asked Luz.

"Yes, of course . . ." Luz began, but Susana didn't let her finish squeaking.

"Never mind," she interrupted. "Just to be sure, I'll count again."

"I'd really like to give her a piece of my

Here's the archaeological site!

Incredimouse!

Wow!

mind!" Pamela huffed, glaring at Susana.

"She's very RUDE," Violet agreed. "And she keeps interrupting Luz as she's talking to the group!"

"It seems like Susana is competing with Luz," Paulina observed. "It's like she's trying to show everyone she's a BETTER guide.

"It doesn't make sense," Colette said, shaking her head. "They're both on the same team!"

At that moment, the group reached a building with remarkable preserved walls covered in marvemouse ancient designs.

"Palacio de Quetzalpapálotl!" Nicky read on a sign as they walked through the building's courtyard.

"I know it seems like a tongue twister!" Luz explained. "But it means 'the Palace of the Quetzal Butterfly.'"

Then she pointed to the bas-relief that

decorated one of the columns in the courtyard.

"It has that name because of the depictions of these **mythological animals** that are half bird and half butterfly," Luz explained.

"**Butterflies** aren't just a symbol of your friendship, but of our trip as well!" Paulina said as she smiled at Luz, Blanca, and Mateo.

They continued to stroll through the city's incredible **ancient ruins** until they reached the foot of the PYRAMID OF THE SUN, one of the largest in the world.

See the bas-reliefs . . .

"Now this is a set of **STAIRS**!" Violet joked as she gazed at the slope to the top.

"It's true there are a **lot** of steps," Luz agreed. "But once you admire the view from the **top**, you'll be glad you did it! **Are you ready?**"

"Let's go!" the Thea Sisters squeaked enthusiastically.

Let's go!

The friends took it one pawstep at a time. Once they had **taken** their last step, they agreed with Luz completely: From the top, the mouselets could feel the sun's positive **energy**!

Meanwhile, Luz showed some members of the tour group a spot at the summit.

"Legend has it that if

you stand right here and make a *wish*, it will come true!" Luz said. Then she stepped aside and let the tourists line up to make their wishes.

A moment later, Susana made a snide remark under her breath, just loud enough for Luz and the Thea Sisters to hear: "I don't think making a wish up here will help you win the competition, but you can try anyway."

Do you want to make a wish?

"I really don't **UNDERSTAND** why she dislikes me," Luz said with a sad sigh to the Thea Sisters. "I try to be *nice* to her, but it doesn't make a difference."

"Maybe you should just ask her," Colette suggested.

Luz didn't waste any time. She approached

Susana as the mouselets watched from afar. But the conversation didn't last long, as Susana quickly brushed Luz off and **scampered** away.

"So, how did it go?" Nicky asked when Luz returned.

"You **saw** what happened," Luz replied, looking disappointed. "She barely let me say a word before she said I was EXAGGERATING and getting worked up over nothing."

Then Luz forced a smile.

"Maybe she's right," she said with a shrug. "I'm better off if I don't think about Susana. I should concentrate on the tourists instead!"

The Thea Sisters watched their friend as she guided the group down the pyramid steps: Luz's attempt to **clear the air** with Susana hadn't worked, which meant nothing about the rude mouselet's behavior would change!

PREPARING WITH THE PROFESSOR

Dr. Meyer called on the evening of the trip to the Teotihuacán archaeological site. The Thea Sisters had returned to Blanca's house and were preparing to sit down to a well-deserved dinner after their long day of sightseeing. They were all looking forward to sneaking in a nap once they were full.

"Hello, Paulina," Dr. Meyer said. "The monarch migration conference begins in a few days! I would like to MEET WITH YOU so we can talk about our presentation and make a plan. Can you and the other Thea Sisters meet me tomorrow at the university convention hall?"

"Of course, Dr. Meyer!" Paulina responded *happily*. "It would be our pleasure!"

"Excellent," Dr. Meyer replied. "This way you can **see** the room where the conference will take place, and you can practice using the equipment as well."

"That sounds `perfect`," Paulina agreed. "And thank you again for the opportunity!"

The next day, the Thea Sisters showed up promptly for their *meeting* with Dr. Meyer at the convention hall.

"Welcome!" the entomologist greeted them warmly. "So what do you think?" She gestured at the room.

"It's a nice room," Colette observed. "And it's really **big**. Do you expect it to be full?"

"I think so," Dr. Meyer replied. "All the RESEARCHERS we invited confirmed their attendance, and the conference is open to the public as well."

"Oh!" Paulina exclaimed nervously. "I

hope my **p h o t o s** are interesting enough."

"Your photos will be a big hit," Dr. Meyer said reassuringly. "Everyone who sees them will feel like they've been **transported** to the reserve. They are the perfect addition to my research. Come, I'll show you around and introduce you to the assistants who will help during the **presentation**."

I'll check it later . . .

While the Thea Sisters followed the entomologist, Nicky's phone **buzzed**. But Nicky thought it would be rude to answer while the professor was showing her and her friends around.

So she left her phone in her pocket.

Once Dr. Meyer had introduced Paulina to everyone, the mouselet felt a bit more at ease.

"Well, now I just have to forget that experts who have studied monarch butterflies for years will be listening, and then I'll be ready to speak at the conference!" she JOKED.

"Don't worry, you'll be great," Dr. Meyer reassured her. "I wouldn't have asked you to accompany me if I wasn't sure you could do it."

Then the entomologist said good-bye and the Thea Sisters left the conference hall.

"What should we do now?" Pamela wondered. "Should we call Luz, Mateo, and Blanca and meet up with them?"

"Oh, that reminds me that I should check my phone!" Nicky said as she pulled it out and looked at the screen. "It rang while we were with Dr. Meyer."

"What is it?" Violet asked, noticing the worried expression on her friend's snout.

"I don't know," Nicky replied. "But judging from that message, it's nothing good!"

¡S ¡T JUST A COïnCïDEnCE?

After reading the message from Luz, the others agreed with Nicky: Something was definitely **WRONG**!

"I wonder what happened," Violet remarked.

"There's **no way** to know," Colette said. "But one thing is certain: **OUR FRIEND NEEDS US!**"

Without wasting a moment, the mouselets headed to the exhibition pavilion and went straight to the stand dedicated to Frida Kahlo. Once they arrived, there was no need for an **explanation**. One look was enough.

"Oh no!" Colette gasped. "What happened to the backdrop you **PAINTED**?"

"I don't know," Luz replied in disbelief, her eyes full of tears. "I don't know what else to say. It was here when I left two days ago, and now it's gone!"

Luz explained that she had arrived at the exhibition hall that morning to work on her **PROJECT**, but when she got there, the panels she had painted with scenes from the garden of La Casa Azul weren't where they should have been! After asking around the exhibition hall to see if anyone had seen the panels, Luz had **TEXTED** her friends for help. Blanca had arrived a few minutes later, followed by Mateo and finally by the Thea Sisters.

"This is just one **mess** after another." Luz sighed. "Up until now, everything can be explained by my lack of attention. But this time I know I didn't make a mistake!"

"Actually, I don't think you did anything wrong the other times, either, Luz," Paulina said thoughtfully.

"So you think someone is **sabotaging** Luz's work on purpose?!" Blanca asked, stunned.

"If just one of these strange incidents had occurred, it might be a coincidence," Nicky reflected. "But too many things have happened."

"That's true," Pamela agreed. "The background **PANELS** couldn't have disappeared on their own."

This one isn't my fault . . .

"Exactly," Pam replied, nodding. "Someone is behind all of this, I'm sure of it!"

"Well, if that's

the case, the saboteur has succeeded," Luz said, sighing bitterly. "It took me months to **paint** that backdrop. I'll never be able to do it again in time for the opening of the **EXHIBITION**!"

"But maybe it is all just a coincidence,"

Mateo cut in. "It's possible the backdrop was **moved** by mistake."

"Yes, it's possible," Violet said. "We don't have proof one way or the other right now, but I know we'll figure out what happened."

Colette put her arm around Luz.

"We **promise** we'll help sort it out," Colette said reassuringly. "We'll FIND your panels so you can take part in the show!"

CLUE!

THE BACKDROP THAT LUZ MADE FOR HER EXHIBITION DISAPPEARED, BUT HOW? LUZ KNOWS SHE ISN'T AT FAULT THIS TIME.

WHAT'S THE PLAN?

The Thea Sisters knew they had to get to the bottom of the mystery of Luz's disappearing PANELS. But they weren't sure how. They needed a plan! So the five Mouseford students left the exhibition hall and found a café with some outdoor tables where they could regroup.

"Let's EXAMINE all the information we have," Paulina said. Then she pulled out a piece of paper with some notes WRITTEN on it.

"Let's go in order," Colette began as she sipped a strawberry *agua fresca*.* "First the hinge came loose from one of Luz's panels. We know Luz assembled the panels in her **exhibition space**, so if someone pulled the screw out on purpose in the hopes that

---

* *Agua fresca* is a refreshing drink made with fresh fruit, water, and lime.

everything would **collapse**, it had to have been done right in the exhibition hall."

"That's true," Violet replied, nodding. "After that there was the strange disappearance of one of Luz's registration forms. But Luz

said she had filled it out, and Blanca and Mateo were witnesses. The papers were definitely in Luz's backpack."

"Right," Nicky said. "Then the folder went missing from Luz's laptop. But the computer was also in Luz's backpack the entire time!"

"And now we're back to the panels, which were here two days ago and are suddenly **gone**!" Paulina concluded.

The friends reflected **silently** as they sipped their fruity drinks.

After a few minutes, Colette finally spoke.

"It's clear that whoever is **behind** this doesn't want Luz to participate in the show, but **why**?"

"Whoever it is must not want to go up against her," Violet guessed. "Luz's work on

Frida Kahlo is really well done, especially because of Luz's unique **artistic** touch."

"If that's why, then everyone participating in the show is a possible **SUSPECT**," Nicky pointed out.

Susana?

"Well, everyone except Susana," Pam said. "She seems to be confident she's going to win. **WAIT!** What if it actually was **Susana**?

"Maybe she isn't as **CONFIDENT** as she seems."

"Susana's work space is very close to Luz's," Violet pointed out. "She had the opportunity to **rummage** through Luz's backpack, and she could have easily gotten her paws on Luz's PANELS . . ."

Colette seemed convinced. "And the panels DISAPPEARED right after Luz and Susana had that little disagreement during the trip to Teotihuacán!" she squeaked.

"Plus, Susana's never been very nice to Luz," Violet said. "So it wouldn't be so STRANGE if she tried to sabotage her during an event as important as this competition."

"She's definitely our number-one suspect," Colette concluded. "We need to keep an eye on her!"

At those words, Pamela suddenly jumped to her paws. "Look over there!" she cried.

The other Thea Sisters FOLLOWED their friend's gaze and saw Susana scampering out of the exhibition hall.

"Let's go, sisters," Violet squeaked, a serious

expression on her snout. "We have to hurry! This is our chance to get to the bottom of this. We cannot let her get away."

A SHOCKING
TURN OF EVENTS!

There was no time to lose: The Thea Sisters left the café and, keeping their distance, followed Susana. The mouselet walked quickly, as if she had to get somewhere as soon as possible.

"Look, she's going down to the subway," Pamela pointed out.

The Thea Sisters watched as Susana scampered onto the escalator that led down to the underground station. The five friends hurried after her, boarding the train at the other end of the car.

Luckily, Susana was busy *FLIPPING* through a notebook, so she didn't notice that the Thea Sisters had **followed** her.

When the train stopped at Coyoacán, Susana hopped off. The Thea Sisters followed her back up to the street as

Let's hope she doesn't see us.

Susana walked quickly through an area of short, **MULTICOLORED** houses. Around them there were a few small stores selling craft items.

"I don't know why, but there's something familiar about this place," Nicky said as she looked around her.

"You're right," Colette agreed. "I definitely feel like I've been here before."

A few minutes later, the mouselets followed Susana around a corner and found themselves in front of a building with ELECTRIC-BLUE walls.

"I guess we know why you feel that way, Colette!" Paulina exclaimed. "We HAVE been here before."

The five friends watched as Susana crossed the **STREET** and entered the Frida Kahlo Museum.

"What is Susana doing at La Casa Azul?" a confused Violet asked. "Do you think it has something to do with Luz's project?"

Pamela shrugged. "I don't know," she replied. "The only way to find out is to follow her inside!"

So the Thea Sisters joined a group of **tourists** visiting the mouseum and watched Susana from afar as she moved from one room to the next. She stopped to carefully study the racks of clothing that had belonged to the **FAMOUSE** painter.

When Susana reached the garden, she sat down at a small table, took out her notebook, and began to write.

"Sisters, I'm feeling a bit CONFUSED," Colette whispered to her friends, who were huddled with her behind some potted plants. "Maybe Susana is just doing research for her own project."

A moment later, Susana put the notebook in her bag, stood up, and headed toward the exit. But Susana didn't notice that her notebook was poking out of the bag, and it slipped out and **fell** to the ground.

"What do we do now?" Nicky asked.

"We get the notebook and give it back to her," Paulina replied. "We can't just PRETEND we didn't see it happen."

She scampered over and picked up the notebook. But when she saw

the contents of the pages the book was open to, she raised her eyebrows.

"**What is it?**" Pamela asked her friend.

"These are sketches of Luz's panels!" Paulina squeaked as she showed her friends the pages.

"Give that back at once!" came a sharp voice.

The Thea Sisters were startled to look up and find an angry Susana glaring at them.

"All right, you found me out," she snapped. "What are you going to do now, tell LUZ?"

That's mine!

"So you admit that it was you?" Colette asked, confused.

"Yes, I admit that I spied on Luz's work," Susana squeaked, sighing. "I know I could have asked her for help, but I'm too **PROUD**. I just couldn't do it!"

The Thea Sisters exchanged **surprised** glances: Susana wanted to ask Luz for help? That was her **SECRET**?

"What do you say we sit down and you explain **everything**?" Violet suggested.

That's how the Thea Sisters discovered what Susana had been up to: She wanted to use some inspiration from Frida Kahlo in her work on traditional Mexican fashion.

"Frida was a style icon, and she often wore traditional outfits," Susana explained. "But I didn't want to copy her famouse **self-portrait** for my project: I wanted to make something really **unique** and **artistic**!"

"And since Luz is an expert on Frida Kahlo and an **artist**, you thought studying her work would help?" Colette suggested.

Susana nodded.

"I really admire Luz," she admitted. "Maybe

that's why I always feel like I'm competing with her."

"But that's a **good thing**!" Nicky exclaimed. "It's like in sports: Competing against those who are better than us pushes us to improve and do our **best**!"

Susana didn't look convinced.

"Yes, but each time I approach to ask her for

Healthy competition can be good!

a suggestion, my **PRIDE** takes over and I end up being mean," Susana explained.

"Well, that's true," Violet said, **SMILING**. "Your way of expressing admiration is a bit strange."

"I think you should try again," Nicky said encouragingly. "I'm sure Luz would like to be your friend, and I know she would be **HaPPy** to help you with your project."

Susana thanked them, and the Thea Sisters felt both **HaPPy** and worried.

It was great news to learn that Susana hadn't been trying to sabotage Luz's project and that she and Luz still had a chance to become **friends**. But it also meant that they were no closer to figuring out who was sabotaging their friend.

They had to start their investigation all over again!

A DISASTROUS DAY

Once the Thea Sisters realized Susana was no longer a suspect, they filled her in on what had happened. Susana was upset to learn about the **mysterious** mishaps, and she offered to help the Thea Sisters with their investigation in whatever way she could.

So while Susana **worked up** the courage to finally ask Luz for advice, the Thea Sisters found themselves in detective mode once more.

"I'm so glad Susana decided to ask Luz for help with her project," Colette told **Blanca** and **Mateo** later that evening. "This way Luz will be busy with something else and she won't be constantly thinking about the missing panels."

"Yes, and in the meantime, we'll do whatever

we can to find them!" Pamela said. "It's not fair that Luz might not be able to take part in the show!"

"What do you think we should do next?" Blanca asked.

"We could go back to the exhibition hall and talk to the other students," Paulina suggested. "Maybe someone noticed something."

"That's a GREAT idea!" Mateo said, suddenly breaking his silence. "I'll come by with the van first thing tomorrow and we can all go over there together!"

The next day, the THEA SISTERS and Blanca waited patiently in front of Blanca's house, but there was no sign of Mateo.

"Where could he be?" Blanca wondered.

Nicky tried to call their friend, but she hung up quickly, a **disappointed** look on her snout.

"It sounds like he's turned off his **cell phone**."

The group of friends waited for almost an hour. Just when they were about to give up and make their way on their own, they spotted the **MULTICOLORED** van in the distance.

"I'm so sorry," Mateo said as the friends climbed aboard. "But the van wouldn't **start** and my phone battery was dead, so there was no way for me to let you know."

"Do you want me to

He's not answering...

How strange!

Here he is!

take a **LOOK** at the motor?" Pam offered. "If there's a problem, it would be better to fix it right away."

"**NO, NO!**" Mateo replied quickly. Then, seeing the **confused** look on Pamela's snout, he added, "We're already late. We better just get going."

Once everyone was in the van, Mateo pulled out into traffic and headed toward the exhibition hall. But a short time later, the van began to **sputter** and came to a stop.

"Oh no!" Colette exclaimed. "**What is it now?!** Is there a problem with the motor again?"

"No, this time it's the gas," Pam replied, pointing at the **flashing** gauge on the dashboard.

Mateo put his paw to his forehead and **GROANED**.

"I can't believe it," he said. "I was so distracted with the motor problem I forgot to fill up the tank!"

"What are we going to do now?" Blanca asked, LOOKING around. "And why are we all the way out here, Mateo? Why didn't you drive through the center of town? That's the quickest way to go."

"I wanted to avoid **TRAFFIC** since we were already late," he said.

"Well, this is one car problem I can't fix!" Pam joked. "We'll have to call for roadside assistance. I'm afraid it's going to be a while."

Unfortunately, Pam was right. More than an hour later, they finally made it to a SERVICE STATION, where Mateo refueled. But by the time the van pulled up in front of the exhibition pavilion, the doors were **locked**.

"Oh no!" Blanca exclaimed, looking at the

hours posted on the door. "They were only open until **NOON** today!"

"It's all my fault," Mateo replied, looking down.

Colette sighed, disappointed.

"It's all right," she said. "We'll just have to try again tomorrow."

"Tomorrow afternoon we have Dr. Meyer's conference," Paulina reminded everyone. "But

we'll have all morning to try to find Luz's panels."

"Hopefully everything will go more **smoothly** then," Violet said.

GOING OVER THE CLUES!

1) THE SCREW COULDN'T HAVE COME OUT OF THE PANEL ON ITS OWN.

2) LUZ IS CERTAIN SHE FILLED OUT THE FORM, SO HOW DID IT DISAPPEAR?

3) WHAT HAPPENED TO THE FOLDER ON LUZ'S COMPUTER?

4) THE BACKGROUND PANELS MUST HAVE BEEN TAKEN BY SOMEONE WHO WANTS TO SABOTAGE LUZ'S PROJECT!

A NEW ANGLE

There were just a few days until the opening of Luz's show, and the Thea Sisters were running out of time to help their friend. Worried that they wouldn't be able to solve the mystery in time, the five friends found themselves awake **super early** the next morning.

"We have an hour before we're supposed to meet Mateo, and Blanca is still sleeping," Pamela pointed out. "What should we do?"

"Why don't we take a walk?" Nicky suggested. "Maybe it will help us clear our heads."

"Great idea," Violet said, and she and her friends walked until they reached a little park. There, they sat on a **bench** and ate some *conchas* — sweet, colorful Mexican breakfast buns — that Pam bought at a bakery along the way.

As they ate, Nicky received a text message from Susana.

"She's sweet to ask for **UPDATES**," Colette observed.

"Hey, wait a minute," Paulina said suddenly. "**Susana** has been spending a lot of time in the exhibition space — we can ask her if she noticed anything unusual around Luz's stand!"

Hi! Work with Luz is going well. Do you have any news?

SUSANA

"I'll call her!" Nicky squeaked. Then she **dialed** Susana's number and put her on squeakerphone.

"Hmm," Susana replied. "I'm sorry, but I

don't remember seeing anything strange."

"Did you see anyone **MILLING** around near Luz's space?" Colette asked.

"No strangers," Susana replied. "Just her friend **Mateo**."

"Mateo?" Paulina asked. "You mean when we were there?"

"Yes, and he was there by himself, too,"

Did you notice anything strange?

Susana said. "The morning after the trip to Teotihuacán, I got to the paVilion pretty early. I saw him there then. I figured Luz had sent him to deliver something with his van."

The Thea Sisters exchanged worried looks and QUICKLY said good-bye to Susana.

"So Mateo was in the exhibition hall the morning Luz's panels DiSaPPeaReD," Pamela said. "But he must have left soon after that, because Luz didn't find him there when she arrived."

"Actually, he got there after Blanca that day, remember?" Nicky pointed out. "Luz called both of them to tell them about the **missing** panels."

"We've been **FRAMING** things wrong," Paulina said thoughtfully.

"Huh?" Nicky asked. "What do you mean?"

"When you take a photograph, you highlight

a detail and place it in the **center** of the frame," Paulina explained. "We had the wrong subject at the center of our **investigation**, leaving the right one in the background."

"You mean we focused solely on Susana and left out everyone else, including Mateo," Violet concluded.

"Exactly," Paulina replied. "We need to approach this from a new **ANGLE**. Mateo had more opportunities than anyone else to sabotage Luz."

The Thea Sisters reexamined everything that had happened and realized Mateo looked very suspicious.

"The morning the screw came out of the hinge, Mateo offered to bring the easels into the room while Luz waited for us outside," Pamela recalled. "So he had the

THE FAULTY HINGE

chance to **remove** the screw without being seen!"

"And Luz said when she filled out the registration forms, Mateo and Blanca were both there with her," Violet added. "So Mateo could have removed one of the **FORMS** from the envelope then."

"And remember what happened in the Chapultepec Forest?" Colette chimed in.

"Mateo didn't want to go boating with us, so he stayed back

THE LOST DOCUMENT

THE FILE THAT WAS ERASED

THE MISSING PANELS

with Luz's backpack. He could have easily erased the file then!"

"Finally, Susana saw Mateo at the exhibition hall by himself the morning the PANELS mysteriously disappeared," Nicky said. "But when he met up with Luz and Blanca, he never mentioned that he had already been there!"

"Great Gouda!" Pamela exclaimed. "This means Mateo may have caused all those problems with the van yesterday. Maybe he wanted to slow down our investigation."

"But why?" Violet asked. "Why would Mateo do this to Luz? She's one of his closest friends!"

"There's only one way to find out," Colette concluded. "We have to talk to Mateo. Let's go back to Blanca's house!"

But when the Thea Sisters got back, Blanca told them that Mateo was meeting them that afternoon at the conference. The mice were hesitant to tell Blanca their **SUSPICIONS** until they had a chance to talk to Mateo.

"I guess we aren't going to solve this STRANGE mystery just yet, sisters," Pamela said when the friends were alone again. "We have a ***busy*** afternoon ahead of us, but hopefully it will also be full of answers!"

AN UNEXPECTED DISCOVERY

The Thea Sisters couldn't think of a single reason why Mateo would want to sabotage his **BEST FRIEND'S** project. But they decided to confront him and get some answers!

"Are you *EXCITED*, Paulina?" Luz asked when they arrived at the conference with Blanca that afternoon.

"Yes, very much!" Paulina replied as she looked around for Mateo. "Is Mateo here yet?"

"No, I guess he's RUNNING LATE again," Blanca replied as she **SAT DOWN** in the audience with her friends.

Soon Dr. Meyer walked onto the stage for her introductory remarks. Paulina popped up from her seat and rushed to the front of the room.

The conference took the Thea Sisters' minds off Mateo for the afternoon: They were so **delighted** by Paulina's photos and her presentation on monarch butterflies, they couldn't focus on anything else!

Blanca, Luz, and the Thea Sisters were thrilled to see the big S M I L E on Paulina's snout at the round of applause the audience gave at the end of the presentation.

"GREAT JOB!" Colette exclaimed, hugging her friend as she got off the stage.

"At first I was so nervous my paws wouldn't stop shaking," Paulina admitted. "But in the end, I could have gone on for hours!"

As you can see from this photo...

Suddenly, the look on Paulina's snout turned serious.

"**Look!**" she squeaked. "There's Mateo! Let's go talk to him!"

"Hi!" Mateo greeted the mouselets. "Nice job, Paulina. Have you seen Luz and Blanca?"

"Yes, but first we need to talk to you," Violet said, holding him back.

The Thea Sisters quickly outlined all that had happened over the past few days and then told him their SUSPICIONS.

"Honestly, we don't understand why anyone would do something like that to a friend," Nicky admitted. "But the more we thought about it, the more the CLUES point to you."

Paulina nodded.

"So we have to ask you a **question**," Paulina said. "Are you the one responsible for sabotaging Luz's project?"

"How could you think that?" Mateo asked as he became red in the snout.

Violet put a paw on Mateo's shoulder.

"Mateo, it's time for the truth," she said firmly. "It was you, wasn't it?"

At those words, Mateo hung his head.

"You're right," he finally admitted, his voice trembling. "It was me. But you don't understand! If Luz wins the contest, she'll leave Mexico City for an entire year. She's always been a part of my life. I can't think of being without her, so I had to stop her."

"I don't believe it!" came a voice from behind them.

The Thea Sisters and Mateo turned to see Luz standing there, a look of **disbelief** on her snout.

"Luz! Please, let me explain!" Mateo pleaded desperately.

"I've heard enough," Luz replied, and then she scampered off in TEARS.

SINCERE REGRET

Mateo tried everything to get Luz to forgive him. First he fixed the background panels of her **FRIDA KAHLO** exhibit. After setting everything up, he added lots of plants that were similar to those in the garden at La Casa Azul, just as Luz had planned.

Then he tried again and again to reach out to Luz by text and email, but it was no use. Luz made it clear that she didn't want to squeak to Mateo. She was too **hurt**.

Mateo sat on the floor in Blanca's living room.

"Do you think Luz will ever FORGIVE ME?" he asked the Thea Sisters.

"Mateo, we've already explained that you need to give her more time," Blanca said patiently. "What you did was wrong and very *serious*. You can't expect her to forgive you right away! She's **hurt**."

"Blanca is right," Colette agreed. "You behaved **badly**, and you betrayed her. She trusted you."

"But I can't wait!" Mateo exclaimed. "Tomorrow is the opening of the show. If Luz wins, she'll be gone for a year, and then it will be impossible to fix things with her!"

I don't want to see him!

"Put yourself in her shoes," Paulina said gently. "Why should Luz believe you if you say you've changed from one day to the next?"

Mateo was quiet for a moment. Then he turned to his friends with a sad smile.

"You're right," he said. "The TRUTH

is, I haven't changed. I'm still scared of losing my friend forever! The only thing that's changed is the reason. Up until a few days ago, I was **scared** at the thought of losing Luz because of the scholarship. But now I'm sad because I know I lost her by being so selfish."

A tear rolled down Mateo's snout. He seemed to have finally realized what he had done to his **dear friend**.

"I wish I could go back in time and **ERASE** all the pain I caused Luz," Mateo said with a sigh.

"**You can't go back**," Violet said. "But maybe we can help Luz leave this terrible mess behind her and convince her that it's time to move **forward**!"

A BUTTERFLY KNOWS THE WAY HOME

The Thea Sisters knew Luz was right to be so upset. But they also didn't want her to lose a good friend forever, if she could learn to forgive him. So they decided to **help** him.

The five friends and Blanca caught up with Luz at the printing shop where she was picking up the final materials for her exhibit at the art show. The friends sat together while they waited for the prints.

"I'm so glad you didn't leave right after the conference and that you stayed in Mexico City until the opening of my show," Luz said.

"We wouldn't have missed this event for anything in the world!" Paulina assured their friend.

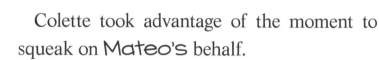

Colette took advantage of the moment to squeak on Mateo's behalf.

"And I know there's someone else who doesn't want to miss it," Colette said softly.

Luz seemed to understand immediately who Colette was talking about.

"If you mean Mateo, I don't want him there," Luz said stiffly.

"Mateo behaved TERRIBLY," Nicky admitted quickly. "He lied to you, he only thought about himself, and he stood in the way of a very important dream. You have every right to be *angry* with him. We would understand if you chose not to forgive him."

"But you should know that he realizes how badly he messed up," Pamela added. "He knows he was **selfish** and that he took the low road."

"We just wanted you to know how much

Mateo regrets what he did," Violet explained. "This competition is about your dream for the **future**. I'm SURE in your heart you always thought Mateo would be part of your future. We just want you to be sure about your decision, that's all."

Are you okay?

"THANK YOU, but I'm not going to change my mind," Luz finally said as she stood up to get her prints. "Mateo **disappointed** me too much. I don't want to have anything to do with him!"

"Well, we tried," Colette told her friends as she joined them outside the store. "Hopefully with some more **time** she'll be able to forgive Mateo eventually."

"Let's video call Mateo and let him know we didn't have much success," Nicky said, taking out her phone.

She opened the video chat app on her phone and called Mateo. But as the phone ᴦₐ𝔫𝔤,

she felt a paw on her shoulder. When she **TURNED**, Nicky was snout-to-snout with Luz.

"Are you calling Mateo?" the mouselet asked.

The Thea Sisters nodded.

"Can I talk to him?" Luz asked as she reached out for Nicky's phone.

"I'm so **ANGRY** at you," Luz began.

Mateo nodded without squeaking.

"But I don't think you know *why* I'm so mad," Luz continued. "It's partly because of what you did, but it's also because you thought I would **forget** about you if I won the scholarship."

"I was scared," Mateo mumbled.

"That's not an excuse. The symbol of our **friendship** is the monarch butterfly, remember?" Luz reminded him. "And monarch butterflies always know how to get home. They may fly thousands of miles away, but their **hearts** never forget the way back."

"So does this mean you **forgive me**?" Mateo asked hopefully.

"No," she said. "But I think I can soon. Now why don't you get over here? Tomorrow is a really important day, and I need my best friend!"

A COLORFUL HEART

The opening of the art show was a real party: Luz was finally able to show off the hard work she had done on her Frida Kahlo project. The event was also a CELEBRATION for everyone who had stood by her those last few days: Blanca, the Thea Sisters, her new friend Susana, and even Mateo, her best friend since childhood.

The announcement that Luz had WON the competition was just an extra reason for joy in a moment that was already filled with friendship and happiness!

"Hooray for Luz!" Mateo exclaimed as he congratulated his dear friend.

"Hooray!" everyone replied.

"So, Luz, are you ready to leave for a year ABROAD?" Paulina asked.

Luz nodded and smiled happily.

"I'm ready to **FLY** away again, just like a monarch butterfly!" she said, laughing.

"And we're ready, too," Blanca added. "Mateo and I studied the university calendar for next year so we can come visit you when we're on breaks!"

"But with Luz leaving, we have one less volunteer tour guide in our group," Susana said sadly.

"No problem," Mateo replied, smiling brightly. "I'll take her place!"

"That's terrific!" Violet exclaimed. "You'll be a great tour guide, Mateo."

"Thanks," Mateo replied. "I really hope I'll do a good job! It will be hard to replace Luz. But I want to help and also make up for all the problems I've caused lately."

"I think that's a wonderful idea," Colette agreed. "Now why don't we all get a GROUP PHOTO together in front of this beautiful backdrop?"

Everyone came together in front of Luz's artwork.

"CHEESE!" the group squeaked happily.

Colette took a look at the image on her phone and sighed softly.

"What is it, Colette?" Pam asked. "Did it come out badly?"

Colette shook her head.

"Not at all," she replied. "I'm just always amazed at the COLORS here. Look at this background. They're the same colors we have on Whale Island, but for some reason everything looks more *vibrant* and beautiful here in Mexico!"

"You're right," Violet agreed. "And the more I look at everything here, the prettier it seems!"

"The best thing about the colors of this trip is that we won't need a **PHOTOGRAPH** to remember them," Paulina reminded her friends. "Because the colors of

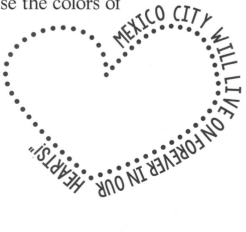

MEXICO CITY WILL LIVE ON FOREVER IN OUR HEARTS!"

Don't miss a single fabumouse adventure!

#1 Lost Treasure of the Emerald Eye

#2 The Curse of the Cheese Pyramid

#3 Cat and Mouse in a Haunted House

#4 I'm Too Fond of My Fur!

#5 Four Mice Deep in the Jungle

#6 Paws Off, Cheddarface!

#7 Red Pizzas for a Blue Count

#8 Attack of the Bandit Cats

#9 A Fabumouse Vacation for Geronimo

#10 All Because of a Cup of Coffee

#11 It's Halloween, You 'Fraidy Mouse!

#12 Merry Christmas, Geronimo!

#13 The Phantom of the Subway

#14 The Temple of the Ruby of Fire

#15 The Mona Mousa Code

#16 A Cheese-Colored Camper

#17 Watch Your Whiskers, Stilton!

#18 Shipwreck on the Pirate Islands

#19 My Name Is Stilton, Geronimo Stilton

#20 Surf's Up, Geronimo!

#21 The Wild, Wild West

#22 The Secret of Cacklefur Castle

A Christmas Tale

#23 Valentine's Day Disaster

#24 Field Trip to Niagara Falls

#25 The Search for Sunken Treasure

#26 The Mummy with No Name

#27 The Christmas Toy Factory

#28 Wedding Crasher

#29 Down and Out Down Under

#30 The Mouse Island Marathon

#31 The Mysterious Cheese Thief

Christmas Catastrophe

#32 Valley of the Giant Skeletons

#33 Geronimo and the Gold Medal Mystery

#34 Geronimo Stilton, Secret Agent

#35 A Very Merry Christmas

#36 Geronimo's Valentine

#37 The Race Across America

#38 A Fabumouse School Adventure

#39 Singing Sensation

#40 The Karate Mouse

#41 Mighty Mount Kilimanjaro

#42 The Peculiar Pumpkin Thief

#43 I'm Not a Supermouse!

#44 The Giant Diamond Robbery

#45 Save the White Whale!

#46 The Haunted Castle

#47 Run for the Hills, Geronimo!

#48 The Mystery in Venice

#49 The Way of the Samurai

#50 This Hotel Is Haunted!

#51 The Enormouse Pearl Heist

#52 Mouse in Space!

#53 Rumble in the Jungle

#54 Get into Gear, Stilton!

#55 The Golden Statue Plot

#56 Flight of the Red Bandit

#57 The Stinky Cheese Vacation

#58 The Super Chef Contest

#59 Welcome to Moldy Manor

#60 The Treasure of Easter Island

#61 Mouse House Hunter

#62 Mouse Overboard!

#63 The Cheese Experiment

#64 Magical Mission

#65 Bollywood Burglary

#66 Operation: Secret Recipe

#67 The Chocolate Chase

#68 Cyber-Thief Showdown

#69 Hug a Tree, Geronimo

#70 The Phantom Bandit

#71 Geronimo on Ice!

#72 The Hawaiian Heist

#73 The Missing Movie

#74 Happy Birthday, Geronimo!

#75 The Sticky Situation

#76 Superstore Surprise

#77 The Last Resort Oasis

#78 Mysterious Eye of the Dragon

#79 Garbage Dump Disaster

#80 Have a Heart, Geronimo

Up Next:

Don't miss any of these exciting Thea Sisters adventures!

Thea Stilton and the
Dragon's Code

Thea Stilton and the
Mountain of Fire

Thea Stilton and the
Ghost of the Shipwreck

Thea Stilton and the
Secret City

Thea Stilton and the
Mystery in Paris

Thea Stilton and the
Cherry Blossom Adventure

Thea Stilton and the
Star Castaways

Thea Stilton: Big Trouble
in the Big Apple

Thea Stilton and the
Ice Treasure

Thea Stilton and the
Secret of the Old Castle

Thea Stilton and the
Blue Scarab Hunt

Thea Stilton and the
Prince's Emerald

Thea Stilton and the
Mystery on the Orient Express

Thea Stilton and the
Dancing Shadows

Thea Stilton and the
Legend of the Fire Flowers

Thea Stilton and the
Spanish Dance Mission